ENJOY
The Ride

L. Stallworth

authorHOUSE®

AuthorHouse™
1663 Liberty Drive
Bloomington, IN 47403
www.authorhouse.com
Phone: 1 (800) 839-8640

Special thank you to Javon Fairley (illustrator) and Xina Sy (editing team)

Published by AuthorHouse   04/06/2016

ISBN: 978-1-5246-0032-7 (sc)
ISBN: 978-1-5246-0031-0 (e)

Library of Congress Control Number: 2016905034

Print information available on the last page.

Any people depicted in stock imagery provided by Thinkstock are models, and such images are being used for illustrative purposes only. Certain stock imagery © Thinkstock.

This book is printed on acid-free paper.

Dedication

I have lost many loved ones. Each and everyone helped mode me into the person I am today. I love you all and none of you could ever be replaced. I dedicate this book to each of you. God put people in our lives for a reason and a season unfortunately our season ended too soon but my life has forever been changed and the moments we shared will never be forgotten. Love you all in a very special way!!

Special Thank You

The Original "Sunday Football Crew" who each one of you continues to support me through everything I do. My ATL family welcomed me back into the family after so many years and introduced me to new family members. The "Get Along Gang" words can't even express how I feel about you guys. Mr. Tilt himself thanks for the laughs and continued support and memories. Last but not least my Chicago family...its all love all the time no other words needed!!

Special Thank You to my Editing Team Xina Sy.

Introduction

There comes a point in every person's life when they need to slow down and take a hard look at themselves. I cannot blame the world for my issues and insecurities. I have had to learn to walk this walk by myself. Having great friends and family is cool; but when you're on the road with nothing but the engine and your own thoughts, then, and only, then can you truly enjoy the ride!!!

Man, I never knew my life in the "A", aka Atlanta, would lead me down this road, but it did; and who knew it would be on two wheels? I'm just a single chick trying to find herself. Funny thing is, I never thought I was lost, until now.

I'm Torri from the south side of Chicago. I am not the typical female. I'm 5'7", not too thick and not too thin, and I have hazel eyes -yes they are natural. I have always been told I have pretty chocolate skin and a pretty smile. I Guess I could drop a few pounds…or 30, but you know women always think we're bigger than we really are!!

I was born to Slick and Baby Sharon. I am from a family of hustlers. When I say hustlers, I mean people who know how to get things done! From them, I learned what I needed to know about the streets and also how to handle myself in professional settings. I know everybody says that, but remember, I did say my dad's name is "Slick". If you don't know who he is then you don't know the Chi!

I left the Chi, aka Chicago, and never looked back. I did the 4-year college thing…had the time of my life, but it was time to move on. I figured I was grown, so decided to move away from everybody and try my luck in the ATL, which is also known as *the land of black hopes and dreams.*

By now, I am supposed to have met a great guy since I have this "good job." Well, everybody says it's a "good job." Personally, I'm bored most days at work. I show up for the 1ST and the 15th! On top of that most people don't even know what I do. They think I work on computers all day…NOT! I have a computer and I do work on it, but I DO NOT work on computers. Hell, when something is wrong with my computer, I call somebody else!

But wait, back to my point. I *should* have a great guy in my life, and we *should* have 2.5 kids with the picket fence and a dog. Somewhere along the way, I must have missed something. I have the house and the "good job", but that's it. Nobody is waiting on me when I get home. No dog, no kids and no man. Sometimes when I think about it, the situation, it can be downright depressing.

But,
This is my story.............

The Start of My Journey

THIS PLACE IRRITATES THE HELL OUT OF ME! Like most people, my job and I have a love hate relationship. I love what I do but hate the pay. I know I can't be the only person that thinks I am over worked and underpaid. What drives me crazy is the fact I can't telecommute. Day in and day out, I sit at my desk in this 10 x 10 cube. It holds me hostage for 8 hours a day. I guess I could be honest considering I take a 2-hour lunch most days it's more like 6 but who really counting?

On my desk sit 2 screens and a laptop. I guess the bosses figure the more screens I have, the more work I am able to do. Actually, it just makes me look busier than I really am. I try to make this space at least look like a piece of an office, but it's not like I have pictures of my kids to put up so it's pretty bare-minimal.

People who I don't like, stop by, and hold long conversations about shit I don't care about. "Speak of the damn devil." Here comes my co-worker Tom (as in Uncle). He is at the top of the food chain when it comes to shit I don't care about. I don't trust this dude as far as I can see in the dark. I would rather trust Stevie Wonder to drive me home on a rainy night. I haven't even had my Starbucks yet, and here he comes. All I hear when he talks is *blah blah this and blah blah that.*

I see this day will never end. I have another boring meeting at 4:30 pm. I guess the people at work know I don't have a life either. Just because I show up every day doesn't mean I want to be here. "My God, this is just a meeting about another damn meeting." I sit in these meetings and see people's lips moving, but nothing is coming out. You know that feeling you get when you know you don't belong in a particular place or just know there's more to life?

I feel like I'm always searching. At one point, I thought I needed another degree. So what did I do? I put myself in more debt and got my Master's Degree. That's right. My dumb self now owes a base model Lexus to Sallie damn Mae. This chick takes all my damn money- along with Wells Fargo and a few other people. When I see her in the streets, it's going to be a problem. In the words of Bernie Mac, "I am going to buss her head to the white meat!!!"

You would think with all my education and free time I would have a lot to keep me busy but the truth is, the single life is not that fun. Married people think the single life is about hanging out and partying. For me, it's actually about watching TV when I'm not working. I am the queen of ratchet TV. They make it, I watch it. I watch it all, from Love and Hip Hop to Real Housewives of Atlanta. The more ratchet the better. What better ways to be distracted from your own boring life then to watch somebody else's? It feels like all I do is watch T.V. and work. I need to find other ways to occupy my time.

Damn, my alarm went off this morning and I didn't even know what day it was. They all run together. Another day full of meetings, listening to people I don't like and talking about shit I don't care about.

"Thank God this meeting is over." I run out of the meeting like the room is on fire, but bad news is on the horizon when I get back to my cubicle. As soon as I arrive at my desk I realize my phone has 5 missed calls and 8 text messages. I can't believe what I am reading. I can't believe what I am hearing. Everybody is telling me to call them; it's important. My messages are from folks who clearly think I already know what is going on. My bestie/hair dresser/sister from another mother was killed in a car accident. I feel numb right now. My mind won't stop. I am trapped at my desk right now looking at this phone. I don't want to answer any calls or messages at this point. I've got to get out of here but I can't move a muscle. I just keep thinking of the last time I saw her. I never thought it would be the last time.

I remember when we first meet....

Like most women, the first thing you do when you move is find someone to do your hair. When you're natural, you just can't let

just anybody do your hair. You got to keep
them ends clipped.

I knew a few folks down here when I
relocated and they recommended Linda. She
was on point too. She was the first person I
actually befriended here in the ATL. She
was a single mom with 2 cute boys. We
clicked right away. She thought I was wild
and vice versa. We laughed about how crazy
men are in the A and how much crazier the
women are.

I saw her every Friday, whether she
was doing my hair or not. She wasn't just a
hair stylist to me. She would have me ride
with her to pick the boys up from school or
baseball practice. She would say I needed to
know where they were so she could send me
some times when she was busy.

I loved that chick. It wasn't a problem
or an issue I had that she didn't know about.
She was a big sister- I could tell her anything
She kept things 100 with me. She was on
board when I told her I was getting my
Master's degree. If I told her about a guy
and what he did wrong, she would check
me really quick. "You gave up the panties
too soon. You can't be mad at him." LOL!!

We had some of the same struggles with men, but she had found her Prince Charming. She even gave me the honor of doing her wedding invitations. She looked so beautiful and happy that day. As she walked down the aisle, she looked at me and mouthed the words, "You're next!!"

God, I miss her! How am I going to get through this? This was not supposed to happen. She has two young boys that need her...HELL, I still need her.

Just when I finally feel like I am getting everything together, this happens. I feel like my heart has been ripped out my chest. I can't focus on anything. I can't stop crying; this is too much! She was my go-to about everything. This hurts too bad. She would normally be the person I would turn to in a situation like this. I have nobody. The feeling of being alone in the world is too much for me to handle. Now what? I have nobody to talk to. I feel like crap; and I need a perm. No wonder I can't get/keep a man.

Life Changing Decision

Gym Time...

I woke up early to hit the gym. I finally decided to go ahead and drop some of this weight. The other day I noticed that my gut was hanging over the waistband of my pants. I never realized how much snack food you can eat when you're depressed. It was time that I switch up the diet and get a real work out plan.

In route to the gym, a guy happened to pull up next to me on a motorcycle. When the light turned green, he took off like a bat out of hell. The roar from the engine turned me on so much, I felt like I should go back home and take a cold shower. Instead, I got my work out on and showered afterwards.

I have been working out a lot since Linda died. The exhaustion I feel after a day in the gym helps me fall to sleep at night. But sometimes I can't fall asleep at all no matter how much working out I do. Some nights I sit up for hours and hours watching infomercial after infomercial. One night, a motorcycle insurance commercial came on. I thought about that guy that left me at the light the other day when I was headed to the gym. Then it hit me...I wanted a bike!!!!! Why not? You only live once. It could be fun riding around listening to that engine without a care in the world. It was official.... I was going to get a motorcycle!!!

So here is where things started to seem real. I realize, on a Google search for motorcycles that, I can't just want a motorcycle because of all the late night insurance commercials, *can I?* The truth is, it seems fun and exciting. So, what do I have to lose? I am single, so why not do something that is different that I can do alone? Little did I know that this one little search is going to open me up to a whole new world!!!

You would think I was telling people I was quitting my "good job" and joining the circus. People lose they mind when I tell them I want a bike. I mean my Granny faxed me a three-page letter trying to dissuade me from my purchase. She actually faxed it. I guess the mailman doesn't move fast enough for her. Even one of my oldest friends, Shannon, is a naysayer. Not just Shannon but the entire "GET ALONG GANG" is going in, you would think they know by now that, I do what I WANT to do. Probably shouldn't have told them all together during lunch. They got stats on bike accidents telling me how dangerous they are and I could die or worst (really what's worse than death?). Folks kill me when they start telling you what to do. Last time I checked all the bills that come to my house; I pay! Well, at least most of them, but they're not paying none of them. It's my life right?!? They don't understand that I need something else…. I want something more. I don't know if the motorcycle is it, but what do I have to lose?

Despite what others say, I did it. I paid for my bike class. That's right, I don't even have a bike, but I'm taking the class. Now I'm on a mission. I've got to find my new toy!! I'm all on Craigslist looking at motorcycles and what not. They make all types. I don't have a clue what the differences are between them. What is a 600cc and a 7500cc? I don't know what I'm looking for, but I know it has to be cute and safe.

The Google has everything. Of course all of my gear will have to match my bike. "Oh snap! They even have cute boots." The boots come damn near up to your knees, but the ankle ones are cute too. I think I want some black boots because I don't think those will get dirty fast. I'm going to need a jacket, gloves and a helmet too. "Lord, what am I going to do with my hair under that thing?" It's all cute and curly now, but after riding around with a helmet, it may not be. That thing may be a problem. I'm also going to need to drop a few more pounds because I'm gone need some cute skinny jeans.

So, I changed my gym schedule and I am now hitting the gym first thing in the morning and lord it's hard. Trying to get into those jeans ain't easy either; and instead of focusing on my goals, I'm focusing on that fine specimen of the male anatomy squatting all that weight.

See this is my problem I can't focus.... MERCY!!! Talk about a tall drink of water. I didn't realize how thirsty I was! I mean, day in and day out, I see this guy at the gym. Arms nice, chest tight, legs on point and I know it's a six- pack under that muscle shirt. Need I say more? How much longer can I continue to see the 6'0 chocolate God without saying something? See, there I go with that focusing problem again. Oh lord, he's coming this way. Suck in that gut. What number was I on? 11, 12, 13…

After a brief conversation, I learn his name is Marcus and his status is complicated. I don't know who came up with that B.S., if you can't check that box on your tax form, then it's not real; but that's not my business!

We exchanged numbers to meet up at the gym sometimes. It starts to seem like from sunup to sundown we stay on the phone; talking and texting. I'm still dealing with not having my girl around and I'm still not sleeping or eating, but I do have this new-found friendship with Marcus. He tells me about his issues and I tell him about mine. I guess Marcus has become my go-to person about everything. If I need my air filter changed I call him or a ride cause my car broke down I call him. I know his situation is complicated but hell; I just need a friend right now, and that is what he is to me. We seem to be able to talk and laugh about everything. I thought I was silly but he wins that battle, hands down. I never thought men and women could really be just friends. I tell him about my drama and he tells me about his. I thought I was a woman with issues, but some of these chicks he comes across got me thinking I am the catch of the year!!!! Why nobody has caught me yet is still a mystery to me!

We've been working out like crazy together. He's got me doing things in the gym I would have never been able to do at this point and I respect his opinion. We have a set workout routine we do most days. We're always talking about our crazy jobs. With him being an EMT, he comes across all types of stuff. One day during our workout I decided to bring up my wanting a motorcycle license. I don't know why I did, but I guess I just wanted his opinion.

Who knew I had a rider in my back pocket all this time? He tells me how he used to ride all the time. He had several different bikes, but he doesn't have a bike anymore, due to his current situation. But again, that's not my business!!!

So, 1 month after losing my best friend, I have this guy that I talk to about any and everything- we are really close. It's like a lost one friend and found another. I feel sometimes that we are meant to be more than just friends, but deep down, I know he can't give me what I need and want right now.

My man drama can wait! I'm not worried about anything because it's almost time for my.... MOTORCYCLE CLASS!!! I got my gloves and helmet ready. I didn't have to buy them either. I got them from Marcus. He has been real helpful lately. He schooled me on all the different CC's and different types of bikes. So I have a better idea of what to look for on craigslist when I get ready to buy. I'm just glad I have someone to turn to about all this. The Get Along Gang still pissed and I don't know anybody else who knows a thing about motorcycles.

My Crew/Family – The Get Along Gang

"*The Get Along Gang*" is a group of friends I have met along the way since I have been out of college. You're always told that high school are the best years of your life, so you figure that is where you will make your best friends. Turns out not to be true. These 3, even though they can tap dance on my last nerve like Sammy Davis JR., mean the world to me. I don't even know how I make it day-to-day without them. I have to seriously thank the Man Upstairs for my second family. I remember how I meet each one of them.

I was starting my first job out of college in a new city, St. Louis. I walked into the training with a brand new business suit on, but I was still nervous as hell. It felt like the first day of school. Each employee went around the room and introduced ourselves… 'Hi my name is…. I graduated from…. I enjoy doing… in my free time.' You know the routine?

Shannon, the statistician of group and one of my oldest friends, seemed like a nice person. We went to lunch together after orientation and just clicked. She thought I was crazy for moving away from my family and everybody I knew. I thought she was crazy because she was about to have a baby. We did everything once she had that little boy. We hit every club up from St. Louis all the way to East St. Louis (IL). We were thick as thieves at work. We were just two young chicks, straight out of college, trying to make our way. Looking back on it now, I thought we were living the life.

When I moved away from St. Louis to Atlanta, we stayed in touch. After some years she eventually moved to Atlanta also and we ended up working for the same company again. I swear it's like nothing had changed except the age of that little boy. We still hang at work and go to lunch together almost every day. Now, well, we hit up clubs in the Atlanta area just a little different since we older…LOL!!

Carter, Carter, Carter…he is the TRUE DIVA of the group. Yes, honey I did say HE!! He keeps us all on point. Every single woman in the ATL should have a TRUE DIVA or a JUDY by her side. I know I love me some him! He is my true ride or die. You mess with one of us, then you mess with us both. I sometimes call him my gay husband. People hate us at work because we're always laughing or smiling, but we always get our work done. It drives them crazy. Between the two of us, we will always have haters ALL DAY LONG!!

The last member of the crew is Jewels. She is the real worker of the group. She is always busy with work but when we finally get her out, she can let her hair down with the best of them She also keeps us in line. We became really close when she was fighting breast cancer. I did everything I could to help her because that is what took my father from me. When I think back on how…

He had pancreatic cancer. By the time we found out he had it, there wasn't much they could do. I wasn't truly able to be there for him because he lived in Chicago. The traveling back and forth was a lot on me, but I did the best I could. I would work all week then drive to Chicago. Spend the weekend and a couple of days up there then turn around and drive back. I did this for weeks. Sometimes I didn't know if I was coming or going. That was my rock. I was a daddy's girl, and watching him act as if nothing was wrong killed me on the inside. Those days with him in that hospice changed me forever.

Although it made me feel better to be there for her, I had doubts to whether or not she would pull through. When you have a front row seat to watch someone you love and cherish succumb to cancer once, it's hard to believe anyone else can, or will, survive. I'm glad she proved me wrong. Jewels showed me a strength I didn't know existed. I watched her fight for her life, not just for her but also for her family.

Now that she's beat it, I swear she is even crazier than before. I think that the chemo killed some of that girl's brain cells though, but I love her anyway!!

Together the four of us have a ball. That's my crew, "*The Get Along Gang.*" Most times when I'm looking for trouble, I am with at least one of them.

I am the only single one in the bunch. They have all been married for years, so I figure that's why they're always pushing me to meet someone. Or, it could be that misery loves company?

Class time...............

I'm glad I'm not the only chick in the class, but the only other chick in here seems really slow. Let's just say she's not the brightest. I hope she gets it together because a bike might kill her. I don't care if it's a 250cc scooter. She needs to pay attention and miss me with the small talk. The *how you doing* and *how long have you wanted to ride* talk. She got my attention when she started telling how she me a cute guy and he rides though. I'm thinking so you riding so you can hang with him? Then she fills me in on how she's breaking up with her boyfriend after this class is over. Ok, wait you got a boo and a boyfriend and *I'm* still single? I can't deal with her problems, though, I need to focus.

We're in this boring ass classroom learning the rules of the road. Hell, I'm ready to ride! They are giving us the basic do's and don'ts of riding like: don't ride alongside a car because you never know when it may change lanes. I never thought there would be special instructions for crossing railroad tracks. Bikers have special hands singles and everything. I should be taking notes. I'm just too excited!!

Day 2………

OMG! I am actually riding this bike! Just around a parking lot, doing 20 mph but hell, I am enjoying this. If the wind feels like this at 20, I can't imagine what 55 feel like.

Riding a bike takes real focus. Every limb is doing something different. One hand is on the clutch and the other is on the throttle/front brake. One foot does the shifting and the other is on the back brake. It is going to take some time to remember all of this. On top of all that, you have to make sure your body position is right going around corners. This a lot to have to remember when I have to look out for minivans and folks texting on their phones as I ride down the street. I should have gotten a bike so I could practice at home! I need to work on throttle control. It's like when you first start driving you can't just lay on the gas pedal you need to learn how to control that. Well, it's the same thing with the throttle. You can't just grab it and take off. This gone take some time but I will get it.

These instructors are crazy. *"Did they just tell me to do a U-turn in a parking space? When will I ever have to do that? Now they want me to slam on my brakes and come to a quick stop?* MERCY! Ok, I'm going to try this, but I don't think this is going to turn out so … goooood!!!

"Oh shit! Did I just fall?" I believe that's what just happened. I refuse to look crazy, so I'm jump up quickly like, "I'm ok… I'm ok"!!

I remember on day 1 they told us they would put you out of class if they felt you would bring harm to yourself or others. Now I am sitting here praying, "Please, oh please don't put me out of class Mister Teacher Man!"

Day 3……

Well they let me come back to class, thank God because Marcus would never let me live that down if they didn't!!! He is always pointing out my mistakes, and he would've thrown this one in my face until the end of time. Wait, this is not about him; this is about me. Again, I'm losing focus.

This day is more fun. We're just riding around in circles, practicing everything we learned yesterday- along with a few extras. I feel like I am catching on, but a bike at home to practice on would have made this day easier.

It is time for the final riding test. I know I am going to pass the written test. Thanks to Miss Question Asker. I got all the information twice…. SMH!!!

I PASSED! It felt good to hear them tell me that. I put my mind to it and I did it. I took a moment and had to remind myself, that the one person I wanted to call… I couldn't. I know she will always be watching over me now cause these folks have let me get a license to ride 2 wheels' baby...YEAH!!

I am ready to hit the road, but I have a major problem...I don't have a damn bike!! I guess it's time to visit my new best friend: Craig, as in Craigslist!!!!

Shopping for a bike online is not easy. These people are trying to sale me garbage bikes. They will put anything on Craigslist. One bike is a Honda in the front but a Suzuki in the back. *"Really, who would buy that?"* I'm glad I have Marcus. He schooled me on everything I need to know, from how to check the tires and the chains. I know NOW, we're thick as thieves.

His friendship is just what I need. We talk all the time. I'm glad we both have AT&T, so we don't have to use minutes. I call him mostly from work. It keeps people away from my desk. I still miss my girl Linda, but it's easier having Marcus around. I didn't think men and women could be this close without being romantically involved, and, apparently neither does the *"Get Along Gang."* They keep trying to make this more than what it is. Sometimes I wonder if they're right.

Anyway, after weeks of calling and looking at bikes I think I finally found a bike. It's a cute orange and black Honda 600cc. It's the perfect starter bike. I'm going to take my cousin to look at it with me. Buying off Craigslist isn't safe, so there's no way I'm going to a strange man's house with $2700 by myself. I'm taking my cousin with me…no way I am letting him kidnap me and turn me into is sex slave. He will have to handle us both!!

When we get to his house, the bike doesn't look as nice as the pictures, but it will do. I decide to buy it anyway, but I can't take it home right at this moment. Silly me I was so excited about the bike I completely didn't realize that I would need someone to ride the bike home for me. So, I decide to have Marcus roll back with me to get the bike. I hope I remember what I learned in class once I get it home…yeah right!

It's been a few months since the class, so true to form, Marcus comes by a few days out the week to help me remember some of the things I forgot. Starting and stopping is an issue for me and Marcus is at my head about it. I come home every day after work and ride around my subdivision. It has become like a drug. I walk through the door from work change clothes and walk right out. I ride that subdivision like its 285 highway going around in circles. I did have a little trouble one day. I stalled out and it wouldn't start. I just knew I broke it. Then I thought, *'oh no the craigslist guy got me.'* He sold me a piece of garbage. I called Marcus upset because I thought something was wrong with the bike. He kept telling me to start it up so he could hear it. I told him it's not starting and he needs to come help. I was close to home but too far way to push it to my house. 20 minutes later I look up and he is riding around the corner looking like he is laughing at me. He got out the car with a gas can. I was so embarrassed he kept laughing and laughing. How was I supposed to know that riding in circles after 3 weeks I would need gas? Then it hit me I never put gas in it before…. LOL!!! Well after all that I think I am ready to take it out for a ride.

Three months later and I finally have this riding thing down. I commute to work mostly, but like I said, it's a starter bike. It is time for an upgrade. Since I know what those CCs are now, I think I want a 1000cc. Size wise the bike is the same it just means it goes faster. That need for speed got me itching like a druggie. Plus, I'm not a small chick, so I need something with more power. I decided to revisit Craigslist, but this time I'm selling *and* buying. I sell my bike in no time. I mean it took a week, and within 2 weeks I found my new baby, a Suzuki. It's a 2006, blue and white GSXR 1000. It is love at first sight. The sound of that loud pipe and that engine purr made me tingle. I now have what I affectionately called, THE GROWN MAN just in time for summer!

My New Boo...Maybe?

As I pull THE GROWN MAN out thinking I'm about to hit the streets, when really I was just going to the post office. I don't do a lot of riding just errands and to work. It's still fun and I love it. This day was different because this car pulls up and a cutie steps out, which of course distracts me from what I was focused on.

This fine man says..." Excuse me?" Do you need some help with that?"

"Yes." I could more than use some help from a tall sexy man getting out of a 2 door black BMW coupe. He is a tall drink of water 6'2, coco brown skin…. MERCY!!! Looked like a tall T.I. and I know I love me some him!!!

So as he tells me his name is Dean but everybody calls him 'D'. In my mind I was thinking does the D stand for delicious?! I will call him whatever he wants me to call him with those big grey eyes. And, people say you need to get out because the man of your dreams is not going to just show up at your door. HA! What do they know? I am standing here listening to him tell me how sexy it is for a woman to ride a bike. What I really heard him say was… WILL YOU MARRY ME?

Fast Forward 2 weeks...

A first date between bike lovers is different. We don't do dinner and a movie. We meet up at a gas station and ride out until somebody gets hungry or signals they need more gas. Since he knows where I stay he is going to come and pick me up. I can't wait to get on road with 'D" and see where the night takes us. What should I wear for the occasion? It needs to be cute and sexy but comfortable. Got to put on the perfect pair of jeans you know the ones that are showing your assets but you're trying to pretend like they don't. The jeans all women have that when they get a compliment on them they say…. "Oh these old things" LOL. Then a cute shirt that if I come out my jacket he will know that outside of riding clothes; I *can* get sexy!

An hour later, he rings my doorbell. My heart automatically falls to the pit of my stomach. I open the door in what I deemed a sexy biker outfit. I have on some tight jeans that show my shape and cute black boots. I have my bandana on to hold my curls in place, but just enough hair coming out in the back so I still look feminine. I also have on a pair of silver loop earrings that will show under my helmet. I know I look dope, because like most chicks, I tried my outfit on 2 days before the date. Once we both checked each other out, I pulled the GROWN MAN OUT. "D" gave me the universal head nod. I threw my leg over that bike and away we rode off.

It's funny, I don't recall ever spending this much time with a man without talking and enjoying myself as much as I am. Most of my riding was around the neighborhood. He had me all over the city. Hours of no communication and it's perfect!

After hours of riding in and out of corners and up and down streets, we finally pull over at a gas station. We sit on our bikes and talk- I mean *really* talk. He begins to tell me about his daughter and how he and her mother were going to get married but it didn't work. He doesn't even give me the, *I got a crazy baby mama speech.* Instead he says that he will always love and adore her for giving him his angel, but a relationship between them wouldn't work. I have to say that I am impressed. I always thought that men like this didn't exist.

As we strap our helmets to ride back home, all I keep thinking is, "Where has he been all my life?" Lord help me! Focusing has always been an issue for me, but I finally seem to have the hang of it. I am focused solely on how to keep this man in my life...by any means necessary!

From this point on, every date is a riding date. We ride for hours, just him and me. We only would ride around the city, until tonight, when he asks me to visit his clubhouse. A clubhouse? How old are you? Really? We have so many other things in common and hang out A LOT. How is it that I never knew he was in a motorcycle club? All this time we riding and you never once told me about a club. What is a motorcycle club really? He was telling me he's been in the club for a while and that he wanted me to come to the anniversary party. I was scratching my head because this was never mentioned before, but I was diggin' him so much. Against my better judgment; I decided to go with him.

This time when he picked me up he had a vest on over his leather jacket. ATL UNDERGROUND STREET RIDERZ is what it read. I'm dressed from head to toe in all black. I make sure I look extra tight and sexy; after all, he is taking me to his clubhouse. This clubhouse thing is strange. I didn't know anything about motorcycle clubs. I've seen them on T.V. in *Sons of Anarchy* but really that was T.V. That stuff can't be real life. Guess I will find out in a few.

The Clubhouse...

This place is nothing special at all. On the outside it looks like an empty one level building. The windows are all black. You can't see anything inside. Looking at the building I was nervous. When you walk inside it's like oh my God! A toy store for grown folks. It's a nice bar on one side of the room. A huge dance floor with a DJ booth against the wall. Then on the other side of the room a couple of pool tables and regular tables. Guess you could say it's a really nice club on the inside with the lights on. Time to party.

I am excited to meet the other club members... until he drops a bomb on me. He explains to me if I think I might want to join the club, it's best we keep our relationship a secret. He goes on to say he likes to keep his personal life out of the club. Sometimes folks can get messy and he just wants our relationship to stay between us.

Ok really?!? Here I am thinking I am all boo'd up and now we have to keep it a secret. We been seeing each other for almost a month now and then you hit me with the secret stuff. Sometimes men will hit you with some crazy shit. I don't care about a club. I only care about him so I guess I can do that. I'll do anything to keep the peace. Now was not the time to fight with him. We rode all the way over here so I guess I have no choice but to conform. I couldn't throw a fit and then have to ride home by myself.

Anyway for the first time I'm hanging with other bikers. I walked in the clubhouse and I swear it looks like a scene from *Biker Boys*! Everybody had vests on, just straight hanging out and listening to music. The DJ was hot and it was like a real anniversary party. Everybody was just hanging around laughing and dancing. People are playing pool and doing their thing. I have never seen so many bikes and bikers in one place. It was real clean biker fun. Just like you see on T.V. I felt wide open. Who knew this could be real life? I felt welcome even though I was an outsider.

All of the bikers have something in common. They consider each other family. They all had nicknames and rolls within the club. They actually answer to these names. One chick was named "Juicy" don't even want to know how she got that name. Then the small skinny chick was "Barbie." The funniest name was a guy called "Six-Eight" his little ass was 5'2" LOL. Your "club name" was supposed to describe you. It wasn't just one club. It was several different clubs at this party. I am new to this world, but whatever it is, I need to be a part of it; so I start to politic. I meet new friends and exchange numbers and before I know it, I have riding partners- men and women. It was strange telling people me and "D" was just friends but I had to do it for him.

There are just as many women riders as there are men. I don't know why this surprises me. The girls open their arms to me, at least most of them anyway. They call and invite me to ride and do different things with them. I finally have something outside of work and the gym. I finally belonged to something! Well, at least, I thought I did.

I can hang with them for most part, but they are a club; and certain things are "club business". Since I'm not a member, I can't be involved in "club business." I still hang and ride with "D" and some of the girls sometimes, but I hate it when he tells me I can't go. I feel like I have a decision to make and it's an easy one. It's time I joined the club. I did 4 years in college and never pledged, but now I want to join a motorcycle club...CRAZY I know!! For the first time I know I'm not alone, like an individual, but like I am part of a group; a family or a secret society that nobody knows about. So I made the decision I will become a prospect for the club. What is a prospect you ask?

> *A PROSPECT is the bottom of the chain. Prospect are supposed to be seen and not heard; so in other words keep your mouth shut. You are never supposed to discuss club business. Your job is to learn about the club,*

> *members and the MC (Motorcycle Club)*
> *community in general. The prospect period*
> *is at least 60 - 90 days. If it goes longer than*
> *that then you messed up somewhere along*
> *the way.*

I spent a lot of time asking questions trying to learn more about the motorcycle community. Funny, as much as I am trying to learn about them they were trying to learn about me. I thought it was my decision to hang around the members to get to know them, but it was really their decision to get to know me. Also, surprising to me, there are more members than I thought. I'm not going to "Club Business" events so some of these people are new to me. I'm glad my "Boo D" is my sponsor. Guess I should break down a sponsor too…

> *Every prospect gets one. You and*
> *your sponsor will exchange all contact*
> *information. Your sponsor needs to be able*
> *to reach you at all times of the day or night.*
> *You will be in contact with your sponsor*
> *multiple times each week. He will be your*
> *primary contact for questions.*

"D" has been telling me things about the MC like the history and rules of the club. I didn't know there were so many rules. Never leave a patch holder (member of the club), never leave your colors (your vest), oh and yes you have to learn everyone's real name; not just their nickname or riding name.

We did a charity event here and there, but nothing major. Most of my time was spent with other members of the club. He told me that at certain events, I couldn't speak to folks. I have to wait for them to speak to me. That was blowing my mind. Motorcycle Clubs are real organizations. I knew they had titles like president and VP; but they have a secretary, sergeant of arms, treasurer, and Road Captain too. They plan for the upcoming year and go over financials like a real company. They support each other *and* other clubs.

There are over 100 clubs here in the ATL. The clubs vary based on their purpose. Some clubs are just for women, some for men. Some are for sport bikes or cruisers. This bike world is bigger than I thought. I am looking forward to becoming a part of it.

Something is just not right...

I have had fun hanging with the club and learning about them, but something isn't right. This chick Nicole is always giving me side eye. She's a prospect also, but I need to figure out what her issue is. She seems like a female that likes to hate on other females for no reason. Not only does she hate on me, but it's a few times she hit up "D's" phone. Now I understand needing help with your bike or having club questions, but really? Something is not right if you calling late at night. Hell where is *your* sponsor? I feel it in my gut. Maybe she's just jealous because I got my Boo and my bike!!

I asked a couple other chicks about her, but they didn't give me anything. I guess that's "club business", hell at this point it's my business because I need the shit to stop. Maybe I will be the bigger woman and sit down and talk with her.

THE TALK.........

I decide tonight is the night I step to Nicole at the clubhouse. When I see her, I do the, *Hey, how you doing... How is everything going thing.* After that, I have to go in because I'm not one for the small talk. Enough is enough.

So I ask her what her problem is with me. Now I kept it in a friendly tone. I didn't put my hand on hip and give her the regular black girl attitude. She gives me this look like I asked about her long lost baby daddy or something. I'm thinking *yes honey I have realized you have an issue with me and I am coming to you asking what it is. I don't play kid games so what is the problem?*

She puts her hand on her hip and pops her lips and gave me black girl attitude but told me, "I don't have no problems with you."

I'm thinking, *that's not true you give me side eye every day and I know you don't look at everybody like that.* Well maybe she does, if so, my bad. I didn't know! I just need to keep it simple and plain. *I don't have any beef with you, so end all this young girl foolishness and act like you got respect for me when I walk by. Let's be honest; we too told for this, so, is that not too much to ask?*

I must have struck a nerve because she removes one hand from her hip and does the finger point to my face and says, "You always flirting with people you have no business flirting with."

She threw me off my square. Who the hell is she talking to with that finger in the air? I didn't know what she was talking about, but clearly she didn't have no home training. She had to know that finger thing would make me mad. I looked at her and said "Bye Felicia."

I turn to walk away and heard her say, You need to stay away from 'D'.

"EXCUSE ME?"

She has now taken 2 steps in my direction and is all up in my face. Talking about he her man and I need to leave him alone. I need to stop texting and calling him all the damn time.

I am lost and confused in this conversation. Did she just tell me that *my Boo* is *her* man? I cleared my throat. "HOLD UP!!! SAY WHAT NOW???"

She calls me everything but Torri at this point. She calls me bitches, whores, and side chicks. It's like I'm standing outside of my body watching everything unfold. I can't take the disrespect anymore. I reach back as far as I can, and in that moment I knew what I was about to do was wrong, but oh well...I slapped the taste out of her mouth!

Before I knew it, I had 3 grown men grab me from behind. As a child I had many fights. I never thought as an adult I would find myself in this situation but something just came over me. It must be all that ratchet TV I watch. Whatever the reason, I was trying real hard to beat her ass. She's going to feel me and remember me in the morning.

Let me be clear, I wasn't fighting over "D". I just never had a woman disrespect me in such a way. I am nobody's side chick!!! I don't know who she thought she was talking to, but I tried to break her damn neck. As for D, I will deal with him later.

Currently they have my ass in another room talking about calm down. I would have calmed down if Ya'll had let me finish whipping her ass. That's a lie I'm getting more and more angry by the minute, because "D" is not here. Where the hell is he? Did he not see what was going on?

Everybody is treating me like I was so wrong. Did they not hear her call me a side chick, a bitch, or a whore?!! When you disrespect somebody, you need to be prepared for the consequences.

Here comes Chrissy. She is like the mother of all the chicks. Guess she coming to get me back in line. She's all in my face telling me how wrong I am and that I need to relax. This is not about right or wrong. She disrespected me. Why doesn't anybody understand that?

I keep texting "D." I'm blowing his phone up, and no answer. Man, when I get my hands on him! He got some chick out here disrespecting me. I knew in my gut something was up. He came at me with that *keep us a secret from the club stuff*!!! I'm calling BULL and SHIT!!

Look who finally comes in the room? I want to yell, holler, and scream at him, so I do everything I can to not look in those big grey eyes. My heart was hurt. He introduced me to this world. I trusted him; only to find out this is who you really are. I just went in on him. "You are a wolf in sheep's clothing. You talk about how you want a man to treat your daughter or sister with respect, but you're not doing that yourself. I'm somebody's daughter and sister. I thought I finally found what I've been searching for, but I was wrong." After that I didn't have much else to say.

The Meeting...

So now we are having a "club" meeting. This drives me crazy. My fate is in the club's hands.

Prospects' fighting each other is not good. And, they're not going to do anything to "D." They'll just tell him to get his shit together. The fact that I might not be in the club is scary to me. Who will I ride with? Losing "D" is hurting, but men are like buses. If you miss one, another will eventually come along.

I can't believe I'm sitting here listening to her say I jumped her because she was dating "D." Really? She really believes that *that's* what it was all about?

Honey you can have him. You got beat down because you called me a side chick. I didn't know Ya'll was seeing each other. While you were texting and calling him, he was in my bed.

He wasn't no fool either, he never left my bed to go see her, but guess on nights he wasn't in my bed. I know where he was now.

His ass is sitting here like he has done no wrong. "Boo if I give you the cookies, we go together. I don't care what you say." I guess I learned my lesson. I will make sure next time I know what we are and where we are headed. Never assume you are the main chick! Can't believe I let myself get caught up. Amazing how your need for love clouds your judgement. People show you who they are and you have to believe them.

New Riding Partner...

The club made their decision. I had to apologize, and my prospect period was going to be extended if I decided to stay. Even though I loved the club, I quickly realized that it wasn't for me. I don't want to be around Nicole or "D." I miss all the club members though. It really was like a family. I had to move on, and she could have him!

I haven't been riding lately and it feels strange. Nobody has hit me up to go riding. I don't know why I expect some of the folks to still be cool with me. The club was like a family and I fought one of their members. It's been rough getting over "D" and the club. Thank goodness I still have my boy Marcus to vibe with. I love our friendship.

Nobody clowns me like he does. I told him about the fight and the club issues. He told me I didn't need to join the club and that I could have just been an independent rider. An independent rider is nothing more than a motorcycle rider who doesn't join the club. However, I did like the club vibe and atmosphere.

He keeps saying he's coming to get my bike since I'm not riding. I told him get his own bike and we can ride together. I guess he showed me because he actually got one, and now I have a new riding partner.

> *I was out once again running errands on my bike and decided to stop a minute. I checked my phone and had a few missed calls from Marcus. I called him and he kept asking where I was. I told him I was out on my bike. He told me to stay where I was he wanted to show me something. I never thought 30 minutes after I hung up that he would roll up to where I was on a motorcycle.*

Can't lie I was really excited. We ride everywhere together now. As always, the *"Get Along Gang"* keeps trying to make something out of our friendship, but I'm cool.

I'm waiting for Marcus at our normal meet up spot, THE TILT, and a cutie rolls up. Like most men when they see me say… "What doing with that bike?" My response is usually the same…"Nothing now but about to ride it!"

He seems like a nice guy. His name is Bryce. Bryce is a cutie with a gorgeous smile. It looks like he whitens each one of his teeth individually. There's nothing like a man with a pretty smile. On top of that, it turns out he rides. He is in a M/C, but I'm not going there. We can date; I might hit up a party or two, but I don't want the club life. I will just have to see how things go with the man…. minus the club.

Really enjoying myself riding with somebody new. Nobody rides the same. Bryce loves to go fast all the time and even though it drives me crazy, I can still keep up.

Marcus has really helped me become a better rider. I lean in the corner like nobody's business. I drag a knee with the best of them. Some days I ride with Bryce, and some days I ride with Marcus. I don't know which one I prefer to ride with. It really doesn't matter as long as I am not riding alone.

Bryce and I are getting closer. He is so sweet. He always checks my tire pressure and oil before we ride. He makes sure my chain is lubed up and everything. When it comes to the bike he will buy me anything. He saw a helmet that he thought would be cute on me, so he got it. My girls Jewels and Shannon think something is up with him, but I keep telling them he just over protective. Of course they think Marcus and I got something going on anyway. I'm so over them harassing me about him. He has a girl. Besides, I am happy with my new BAE.

Despite our relationships, Marcus and I still manage to spend plenty of time together. Today we are hanging out at our usual rendezvous point. We're chillin, and guess who rolls up in his car? BAE. It felt strange introducing him to Marcus.

Before I could tell Marcus his name, he extends his hand and introduces himself as "NoLow," his biker name. I was really wondering what that was about.

When we walked away from Marcus, for some reason Bryce had an attitude. Something was different in his eyes and that big vein was popping out of his forehead.

He didn't have that sweet look anymore. His attitude was very strange and I planned on finding out what was going on with him.

I'm finally back from riding with Marcus and there are 8 missed calls from Bryce. So I called him back because it was very clear he was definitely a little testy earlier.

He came with *the where you been and what you been doing* conversation. I was scratching my head because you just saw what I was doing. I told him Marcus and I was out riding but I was home now. He told me he was on his way and hung up the phone; no bye or nothing. SMH. Men are so sensitive sometimes.

I didn't even get a chance to wash my face, and here he comes knocking on the door like the damn police. His attitude was definitely on 10. It took him like 5 minutes to get to my house, which was strange cause he lived 15 minutes away.

He starts out with the, *"You out with another man on a bike. How you think that look?"* He goes onto explain that he is in a club and I have been around his club members. I need to understand that was not a good look. I am *his property* and I can't be riding with another man.

"Excuse me. PROPERTY????"

> *"So in MC world, when a woman is dating or married to a guy in the club she will wear a patch that says Property Of?" Yes, that's correct. Property Of. It really means that that woman gets the same respect and protection as her man in the club.*

Now that shit is crazy to me because I don't have a patch on none of my gear. Last I checked I just go to the parties with him. I had no clue about being his "property."

I try to reason with him, but he is really mad. I guess he has a jealous streak because I have never seen him so upset. Now would not be the time to ask why he didn't want Marcus to know his real name. I'm going to take the back seat in this conversation and just nod and agree. I do need to make it clear to him at some point that I am not anybody's property. I can and will ride with whoever I want whenever I want.

I finally convince him that Marcus and I are just friends. Men trip over some of the littlest things sometimes. It took a while but I explain that Marcus has a girl. He's not checking for me at all and I am happy with you, so no need to worry.

Things between Bryce and I are getting better. He comes over more often and we ride together all the time. I have no time to ride with Marcus because Bryce and I are always together now. It is great how he loves spending time with me. But I have to admit the constant calling and checking on me is a bit much. Every woman wants a man that is really into them, but DAMN can I even pee in peace!?!

Bryce can be so cute sometimes. He even gets jealous when I got plans with the *"Get Along Gang."* He calls me before we leave and texts me while I'm out. He comes over as soon as he knows I'm back home. Of course the crew always have something to say. They just don't like him, but it doesn't matter because he loves me.

I miss Marcus sometimes, but we still chat on occasion. I would like to speak to him more often, but Bryce really does control most of my free time.

Although I enjoy my time with Bryce, some of the strange things he does when he comes over are really starting to get to me. For instance, he goes in the garage and checks the GROWN MAN to see if it is warm even after I told him I haven't been out riding. One day I came home from work, and my bike was gone. He told me he was getting it painted. That took almost 3 weeks but when the GROWN MAN came back he got it painted purple, his club color, *and* got me a purple Curvy Riderz Corset jacket to go with it. Don't get me wrong, the jacket is sexy as hell and the bike is nice, but purple is his color, not mine. I was giving him the side eye but I appreciated the thought…I guess?!?

As he comes in from the garage one day checking my bike I just went ahead and asked him what that was all about. He said, "Just making sure you not riding with dude." I'm like, *by dude do you mean Marcus?* It's like he doesn't trust me. I was telling him he can't control me and I will do what I want with whom I want.

He steps two inches too close and says, "If I find out you been out with that Marcus, you gone have problems!!!"

I'm gone have problems? The way he said that didn't sit well with me at all. I was thinking if he got that close to me again, with that attitude *he* was going to have problems. Something in me told me not to say that. I have never been scared of a man before but that look in his eye told me something wasn't right. I can't be with someone I am scared of and in this moment I was scared. All the things the "*Get Along Gang*" were saying might be true. He was controlling and jealous and that was a bad combination. In this very moment I had to agree with them.

Right away I know I have to get out of this relationship; he got me twisted. I put up with a lot of things, but having a man tell me 'I'm gone be in trouble' like he gone beat my ass, is not one of them. I decided to stay cool and plan my escape. I didn't know how to do it. I didn't want to make him mad because clearly he was nuts. I did what seemed best and most logical. I slowly moved away. I got busy with work and limited my free time with him. True to form he had an issue but I was never alone with him to express it. The few times he tried to come over I always had plans with the "*Get Along Gang*". He snapped a few times and I just stayed calm.

I no longer answered his calls; I changed my locks, and as far as I am concerned, Bryce, aka, "NoLow" and his club are dead to me!!! I eventually pulled a *Houdini* on his ass, and disappeared.

One wrong turn...

Phew! It took a while but I finally got him to leave me alone. I still double check, my surroundings when I walked out of any place and triple locked my doors at night and jumped when I heard the wind blowing through bushes. It's a damn shame that I was that paranoid.

The *"Get Along Gang"* was right about him. He has more issues than *Sistah to Sistah* magazine. I didn't know if he would have ever hit me, but lord knows I wasn't taking any chances.

I'm currently back to not having anybody to ride with because Marcus' "girlfriend" got a bike, so there goes that. We still talk all the time on the phone though. I feel like that will never go away.

I hate that all I have right now is work, home, and the gym again. It's weird cause I miss Marcus. We get out sometimes, but only when his "girlfriend" can't ride. This Saturday, I plan on riding alone. Normally I just run errands but this time I'm going to do a *real* ride. It has been a while since I really rode my bike by myself. I mean, I have bent a few corners alone, but never really putting it down like when I'm with other riders.

This day is different. I hit 120 mph for the hell of it, and it felt liberating! It was a great ride there until I made that left turn. My eyes widened, my tires screeched and everything started moving slow, but fast at the same time. A car stopped in front of me. My eyes closed and the next thing I saw was the blurry blue sky. Then it was completely black!

This is where my memory becomes super hazy. There is a lot about that accident I don't remember. People tell me that I never blacked out. I vaguely remember talking in the E.R. and trying to remember how I got there. When I felt that pain go up my entire right side I quickly remembered….my dumb ass fell!

After what I imagine to be hours later, my eyes flicker and I wake up. Surprisingly, I feel no pain. I was in that big room surrounded by all my friends and some people in white coats. I try to raise my hands up, but it feels like I was being stabbed in my wrist. I want to scream out but I don't have the strength to open my mouth. The nurse that tends to me told me that I broke my wrist and my leg. I just kept thinking, "Who is going to take care of me?" #singlegirlproblems

Looks like I had nothing to worry about. My crew has come through for me. I mean they have a schedule around the clock for me. Marcus made the shifts. They tease me about him all the time, but they made sure to include him in the rotation. Shannon – handles the coordination; Carter sends a cleaning guy over; and Jewels handles food and meds. Marcus's job is to keep me in good spirits. I can't do anything for myself. This sucks! I can go to the bathroom alone, but even that's a struggle. Jewels did offer to hire a nurse to give me a bath because she, *"don't wash ass."* LMAO!!! This experience has made me realize how much my crew cares for me.

Marcus told me he was coming over so I figured now would be a good time to try and wash my ass before he got there. I hear Marcus knocking on the door while I'm in full wash-my-ass-mode. The only problem is that I'm not doing a very good job. I'm washing, and he is ringing the doorbell like a crazed delivery boy who wants his tip. I grab the phone to call him.

He's yelling like *why you not answer the door...*how do you explain, *because I got one leg up and a bag on one hand trying to wash my ass.* I explained to him I am temporarily handicapped and I was having trouble finishing my bath, so, getting to the door was an issue right now.

I look in the mirror and I look crazy for real. Soap is splashed all on the mirror and on my face. This half-ass attempt to bathe is a complete failure. I reached for a robe and hobble my handicap butt to the door. He was talking about he's only on a break for an hour.

When I open the door, Marcus looks at me like I was a fool.

I explain to him how I was trying to give myself a bath and as I look up he just won't stop laughing. I don't know what's so funny but truth is when you think about it, it's kind of funny. I got one good leg and one good hand and I'm trying to wash my ass.

The next thing I know; he is grinning from ear to ear. Talking about if I need help washing my ass as a friend he can step up to help. Truth is he really could help being he is an EMT. I gave him a long look and felt like this has got to be crazy but truth is I needed help and he was there!!

Now Marcus's sole purpose in the rotation is to bathe me. It's amazing how close you get to someone when they have to help you wash your ass. Sometimes it makes me feel weird. We have deep, intimate conversations with ease; I guess confiding in him has gotten easier since he has seen me naked. LOL I will never admit it to the "*Get Along Gang*", but I think I do care about him a little more than just a friend.

Week after week Marcus comes over. We laugh, joke, eat together, and watch Sports Center and then he helps me wash my ass. What has my life become?

I can't believe I have feelings for someone who is with someone else. I want to tell him, but I can't become one of those chicks. The type the independent girl, who appears to have it all together, but becomes a side-chick because she gets caught up. Really, I can't be her. I just need to get my emotions under control. But to be fair to myself, he doesn't know how I really feel. Maybe he could feel the same way…

I couldn't keep letting him come over and help me bathe knowing I had feelings for him. So I had my cousin fly down to help me get around and other stuff. She's a trip. Having her around has been great, until she started siding with the "*Get Along Gang*" about Marcus and I. I guess she got that vibe because Marcus still comes by and hangs with us all the time.

Dealing with my injuries is hard enough, dealing with my feelings for Marcus is even harder. I think about him ALL the time. THIS SUCKS!!! I'm stuck in the house and he's out riding with his girl! Between the thought of them riding together and my broken body, I don't even know if I want to ride again.

It's been 10 weeks. My casts are off, my cousin is gone, and I'm back at work. The first person on my doorstep was Marcus. Talking about how nice the weather is and we needed to ride.

I wanted to slam the door right in his face. Ain't no way I'm getting back on a bike after I flipped and broke my wrist and my leg. Like I want to ever do that shit again.

I explained that I wasn't riding anytime soon since the bike is all messed up now.

Marcus has a smug look on his; he was not going to let me off the hook. He always has something to say. I swear this dude thinks he knows what $E=MC^2$ actually means.

He tells me about a shop where a friend of his works. Truth is, I wasn't even thinking about getting back on that bike. I'm all up in my…**FEELINGS.**

I had all the excuses in the world. I am as tough as they come and as strong as anyone, but hell that damn bike scared the shit out of me. Plus I got a $500-dollar deductible to get my bike fixed.

Last thing I need is to report this to my insurance company. I got that ticket blasting up 85 North. That's what I get thinking I could keep up with the boys…

know damn well I don't like blasting. I didn't run from the police my goofy ass pulled over and got the ticket.

Marcus cut me off so fast. If I take a small breath in conversation, he thinks it's an invitation to tell me what he thinks. He told me have it towed to his guy's shop and he would hook me up on the labor and parts.

In the back of my mind I wanted to just tell him I'm done with riding. I know when the winter comes my wrist and leg is going to hurt. I'm going to feel like an old man with arthritis, predicting when it's going to rain and shit.

The truth of the matter is the physical pain is not my true concern; it is the mental aspect of it. When I first started riding the thrill was being able to control the power and the speed of the bike. Now I fear those things. If I admitted I was scared, Marcus would clown me.

I'm like look Marcus, it's going to cost $3000 out of pocket to fix the bike. Hell, it cost $15000 to fix me. I'd rather just let the bike be for a while.

He goes on and on about how I sound scared. I'm being a punk; and how it's like a horse you fall off you have to get back on. Why in the world did he have to say that to me? I lost it!

Maybe I am scared; So what! I flipped off a damn bike. I broke my wrist and leg. I could have been killed; and he wants me to just bounce off the ground and get back on the bike. I could hear myself shouting but, I had to tell him, *how about you man up and let your girlfriend know you don't love her -or are you scared?*

I don't know what came over me. Maybe I lashed out because he gets under my skin like a fungus. Maybe

I was jealous. Maybe I miss Linda…maybe I'm scared. Whatever it was, Marcus got all of my frustrations for 10 minutes straight. He was just trying to be a friend.

At that moment, he looked at me and without a word; put on his helmet; and walked off. When he started I wanted to scream for him not to go, but it wouldn't come out.

Confessing how I feel...

I woke up to get a workout in and hopefully to see Marcus. I wanted to apologize for the other day. I know I was wrong- and right at the same time. I was wrong because I should not have lashed out at him the way I did, but I was right by telling him he was scared to address his relationship issues. We talked about everything and he had been telling me for a while he wasn't happy. He's always talking about life lessons; I guess I felt I needed to give him one. He is always really quick to call somebody out. Men kill me. They always saying women are always in our feelings, but they get in theirs also. I just need to apologize.

Once I arrive at the gym I go to the area where I know he usually starts his workout. No luck there, so I go to the cardio area. For some odd reason, I'm really not feeling the gym. I try the stationary bike, but I'm just not into it. So I hop on the treadmill for 30 minutes to walk and get my wind back. I just know he is going to show up at any minute. 3 minutes on the cool down and still no sign of Marcus. I keep the workout going, but the truth is my heart isn't in it. I decide to extend my time in here, so I decide to try my luck in the strength and conditioning area. Unfortunately, Marcus never shows. This is not like him at all!!

The next day at work I replay, in my mind, how harsh I was to Marcus. I am driving myself crazy. This not talking to him is killing me so I figure I should send him a text. I know things in texts can be misconstrued and the worst thing that could happen is I text a long apology and he just texts me back "ok", that is murder in text land. I decide to re-read the text before I hit send.

> *I know I was very mean to you the other day, but I want to apologize. I hate doing it this way and I would rather do it in person. Please know that what I said was coming from a place of love.*

I push send it gets delivered at 10:02 am. God I hate texting somebody waiting on a response. Maybe I shouldn't have sent it. Maybe it didn't go through. Maybe something's wrong with his phone. I need to relax. I just sent it. Its only 10:30. Well whatever, I made initial contact now let me get my ass to the meeting.

Right on cue here is Tom asking if I am ready for this meeting. Hell I'm never ready for these meetings with chatty Tom. Hell, I don't need this meeting. Tom's always scheduling meetings to make himself look busy and I hate that.

Tom *blah blah blahed* me until we got into the meeting. I thought we were early, but the room is filled to capacity. Apparently, there are some new systems we need to learn. As we sit in the meeting I glance at the clock wondering if Marcus texted me back- I left my phone in my desk and I have to wait to find out. I know the only things he would text me back is one of his 2 favorite words, *Word or Trill*. Word/Trill can mean, 'Yeah, you're right' or 'You're full of shit.'

I can't wait for this meeting to end so I can check the phone for my message from Marcus. I go to my desk immediately following the meeting. I am excited to see I have 3 text messages. I was thinking maybe Marcus does love me! I soon realize that the three messages are from Jewels. Apparently while she was having lunch at a downtown restaurant, Marcus showed up with his girlfriend. My face drops as I read the news. I don't know why I am having such a strong reaction. It isn't like I didn't know he had a girl. This is too much. I'm just going to leave him alone and concentrate on figuring out these new systems for work.

I have a lot going through my mind. I definitely need to apologize; and at some point, I have to tell him how I feel. He is always telling me how bad his relationship is, so maybe I can tell him how I feel and see what happens. This caring for somebody and not knowing how they feel is hard. Everybody thinks he has feelings for me because he is always around, but I have to remind myself that he's in a relationship. I think I'm just ready to ride again but riding solo after going down is scary. Once I get my bike back maybe my fear will go away.

I'm sitting here reflecting on how my last few relationships have gone bad- and fast. I mean with D, he lied and then I found myself fighting some chick. Bryce was so controlling and jealous it scared me. He literally wanted to know my every move. That fool damn near wanted me to answer the phone while I was riding. Now I am crushing on Marcus. I have no idea how this one is going to turn out.

Marcus finally texts me back. His reply, *Word,* did not surprise me. Took him all day to text me back that one damn word. What did surprise me is the text that I got five minutes later. Marcus is finally on his way over to my house. He is going to drop off my bike. I think it is time I tell him. I feel sick to my stomach. Why is this so hard?

HERE I GO…

I took a deep breath and began, "I have dated many men. I've been doing this since I was 16, and I have never had a relationship with a man like the one I have with him. This guy has become my best friend. I feel like I can share anything with him and what I want to share with him most is my LIFE." Saying all this felt weird… the way he was looking made me even more nervous but I was in it so I continued, "I know you have a relationship but let's be honest, it's not what you want. I think we both deserve better than the people we have been with and I think we could be good for each other. The foundation of the friendship will only make our relationship better. The way you took care of me after I went down and have been by my side just makes my feelings stronger."

Once I got all that off my chest we both sat there for a minute. It seemed like hours in silence but it was only 90 seconds. He told me, *he loves our friendship and he never wants to lose it but he has somebody in his life and things are going good.* Wasn't much I could say other than *Word*!!

Deep inside I don't know how to feel. I just poured my soul to this man, and it fell on deaf ears. I guess he doesn't care about me the way I thought he did. To add insult to injury, here I am with this gorgeous newly painted bike and nobody to ride with. Man this sucks.

Marcus still comes around but it's awkward. He has emotionally checked out. Despite the cold shoulder he's giving, the "*Get Along Gang*" insists that he has feelings for me. They think he's just confused. What do they know? He said he's not interested. I need to move on. Right?

What next...

Every day after work it's the same routine. I pull into my garage, get out my car, and walk past my bike like it doesn't exist. I have no desire to ride. The thrill is gone. I walk in the garage and there is the GROWN MAN, looking at me. It's like he's saying, "You just gone keep walking by and not even start me up?"

I stood there looking long and hard at him. I remember when a day wouldn't go by that I didn't jump on him. I would ride The GROWN MAN to my mailbox at the end of the driveway if I could. It's crazy how times have changed. It wasn't about having a riding partner it was about conquering my fears. I just can't pull myself out of this funk. It is the littlest things that can pull you back into a depressive state. Now when I look at the GROWN MAN, I don't think about riding; I think about chocolate ice cream and hot wings.

I don't think I'm just dealing with my feelings for Marcus, I think I am still missing Linda I need to hear her tell me to shake it off and get back on that GROWN MAN!! The "*Get Along Gang*" all wants me to hang up my helmet. Deep down, I am starting to agree with them, but then again I'm not ready. Linda would have never let me reach this point. She'd slap me in the back of the neck and tell me I was tripping.

I haven't sat on the thing since Marcus brought it back. I am looking for any excuse not to ride. Thank God Shannon is calling me to come out for drinks. That is exactly what I need. She said the *"Get Along Gang"* is going to meet at the bar for happy hour to celebrate Jewels' birthday. I've been so deep in my own problems, that I completely forgot. I need to stop and get a gift card or something. Man I am slipping. A stiff drink is exactly what I need!

When I arrive at the bar, everyone is here, and the $5 drink specials were flowing. Everyone is also boo'd up. I don't know why, but they can't seem to resist throwing shade about me not being on the GROWN MAN- especially on a gorgeous day like today. I can't respond, I'm just going to sit here and continue to give them all side eye.

They know I don't drink and ride. I'm already feeling some type of way about everyone being there with their Boo and all the bike talk.

They're all going back and forth...I should be on it because it nice but I need to hang it up because it's not safe. Right now I feel like I can't win for losing!

Everyone else is having fun. A few guys tried to holla, but I'm not feeling that right now. It's time for me to head home. I thought the drinks and hanging with the crew would help but it didn't. I am still messed up emotionally.

As I pull into my garage, it seems as if the sky bottomed out. Just as I begin to admire the rain, I get a call from Marcus. He's just checking on me, wanting to see how I'm doing. Really you know how I am doing. I don't even feel like going there. He wondering if I have been riding and I didn't want him to go in on me but I told the truth and said NO.

He tells me I need to go with him on a ride down to Savannah with him tomorrow. His cousin is having his annual barbeque. It's supposed to be a big deal. Family and friends from all over come.

In my mind I was thinking "Hell yeah", but I had two issues: I'm gun shy about riding and why is he not taking his girlfriend?

He tells me they had a fight and he not trying to miss this because of her. I was thinking he knows I would be more fun anyway.

I agreed to go but I swear I was having second thoughts. Then again I was so excited that I laid my outfit out as soon as we got off the phone. I pulled out my Curvy Riderz Jacket, a cute little shirt and black jeans. I had to make sure I was looking extra sexy. I am looking forward to riding out with him. The truth of the matter is; I don't know if I am excited about riding or riding with him.

Road Trip....

I feel energized this morning. I text Marcus to find out what time we're taking off. He texts me right back and say to be ready at 1pm. I am cool with that because I have time to get my lashes and hair done before we leave. Even though I am excited about our ride I am a little uneasy. I feel like I'm disrespecting his relationship in some way. I really shouldn't feel that bad because he knows how I feel, and yet he still asked me to go with him.

It's noon, and like TI said, *'get your hair nails done get your shit together',* so I did just that. I'm still waiting on Marcus to hit me up. I shoot him a quick text to let him know I'm ready. 30 minutes go by, no response. I don't want to blow his phone up, but I am starting to become concerned.

When I call his phone it's going straight to voicemail, so I figure he's headed my way. Then I thought he has a Bluetooth headset, so why is he not answering?

It's now 3:00 and no word, no call, no nothing. All types of crazy things are going through my head. I check FB because bike groups normally post if somebody has gone down. I didn't see any posts. Do I call hospitals in the area to see if anybody has come in from a motorcycle accident? I was tempted to call his mother, but I didn't want to worry her. He has never gone missing like this without any word. He could be in a ditch somewhere bleeding to death. I don't know what to do.

Now who's apologizing...

I wake up to about 15 messages from Marcus apologizing. It's too little too late. At this point I'm done. He had me sitting around waiting on him and now he wants to apologize. I'm glad he's not dead, so I still had the opportunity to kill his ass. I've never been stood up. I feel so disrespected. Here I am getting emotional and I'm not even with him.

Let me quit tripping. Maybe something happened to his mom or something. I don't want to fly off the handle so I am just going to go to the gym and work out. I need to calm down. In fact, I'm going to ride my bike to enjoy myself.

Men kill me saying all the stuff they want from a woman: independent, attractive, cook, clean, no kids etc. When men have all of that in front of them, they choose the woman with issues and that are needy and unstable. They love drama; they just can't admit it. He thinks he can stand me up? Yeah ok!! He has no idea the enemy he has created.

I put on my work out pants look at myself in the mirror. I haven't noticed how thick and curvy I was in a while. I have been spending so much time stressing over men I haven't even noticed how much sexier I have gotten with all these gym workouts. No man in his right mind would stand up all this *lusciousness.*

The moment I start the GROWN MAN and heard that engine, all my anger disappears. Riding through my subdivision, I realize Marcus standing me up was something that I have never experienced in the past! I pull up in the gym and it was a few bikes already there. One of them appeared to be Marcus's bike.

I sit on my bike for a few seconds trying to fully digest what was going on! I never would normally work out on a Sunday. The weekends are my rest days. I decide to go workout, and if I see him, I will keep it pushing. As I get off my bike another text message comes through, *So you really not going to talk to me? I'm really sorry.*

Just then he comes out the door. When he sees me he looks like he has seen a ghost.

In my mind I plan on speaking and keep it moving but he wasn't going to allow that. He explains how yesterday was his fault. Like duh who else's fault could it have been?

He talking about they made up and he couldn't really reach me. REALLY? Funny how he could reach me to ask me to go, however he couldn't reach me to cancel.

He realized I wasn't really feeling his apology but he went on about how he thought about it and couldn't disrespect his girl but he didn't mean to hurt or disrespect me in the process. I was thinking, *dude it was a barbeque either you wanted me to go or not.*

Here we are standing outside the gym and he is telling me, *yeah we have issues and all that but whatever she still my lady.* I wasn't in the mood so I gave him the one word of death from every woman…." OK!"

The word 'ok' has several different meanings. I gave him the one that means *Don't fuck with me right now because I will beat your ass!!*

I just realized he wasn't who I thought he was. A real man makes a decision and lives with it! Standing me up was a bad decision. I know women like me come along once in a lifetime. This guy is just going to miss out because he got me twisted thinking I am going to sweat him. I don't know why this hit me so hard. I told him to delete my number. I know deep down I have feelings for him but since I can't have him I need to move on.

Out of the corner of my eye, I see a woman skipping out of the gym and over to Marcus. She kisses him on the cheek.

She gives me the *this my man look*…If only she knew. I know more about their relationship then she does. I fix my face and say hello and walk away from the both of them- I kept my composure until I made it into the women's locker room. I headed straight for a stall and cried my eyes out.

I feel like I have so much more to say. I sat and listened to him complain about her day in and day and here they are looking happy. I'm so mad at myself for getting excited about going somewhere with him. I can't even concentrate on working out right now. I clean my face and head home. I didn't get my workout in today, but I feel like I lost 198lbs!! Having feelings for someone you can't have is hard but holding on to it is even harder.

Solo Ride...

Week after to running in Marcus I think it's time I venture out on my own again. I have this bike so that I can do me, so I need to do me.

I use to call my grandfather before I would take a long ride with Marcus, so I decided to keep with that tradition. I hit up my favorite old man and told him I was about to go riding. I couldn't bring myself to tell him by myself. I didn't want him to worry about me.

I forgot how much fun this is. I'm hitting corners, highways, and long roads like I used to. I even hit the mountains. I'll hit 285 Hwy tomorrow morning around 5. I know some people might say that's crazy, but Lord it felt good to watch the sun come up on 2's.

I often look back on why I first got this bike. It was really to do something different and to make a change in my life. I have done that. Since having this bike, I have met some interesting characters. Men I thought would be with me forever and women I thought would hold me down.

I have come a long way. Before my fall-out with Marcus, I enjoyed riding, but I never rode alone. Errands don't count. I mean really just ride until I need gas… alone. I always had some man with me. When did I become *that* girl? You know the chick that is always with somebody, but truth is she's never really happy by herself. She allows her happiness to come from being with a man. SMH!! I don't know when it happened to me.

I was all into "D" he showed me a whole new world. I didn't know about clubs and clubhouses. The anniversary parties were off the chain. Those were some of the best parties I ever went to.

Then there was Bryce…really?! Never thought I would lose myself in such a controlling asshole. I think he was one night away from putting his hands on me, and I couldn't have that. I did get a nice paint job on my bike and a sexy Curvy Riderz Jacket out of it.

The one man I truly loved was Marcus. I do miss our friendship. Our rides were always the most fun. Not because of the adventures we had, but because of the talks we would have afterwards. But alas, I am finally enjoying, I mean truly enjoying, this ride by myself.

After a long ride, I pull up to The Tilt and who rolls up but Marcus. Even though it has only been one month I told him to delete my number, it seems like it has been ages. After that gym blow up I guess he really did delete my number. Hell I changed his contact to DO NOT ANSWER and took time to deal with my feelings.

He rolls up and speaks like we were still Best Friends. I figure, what the *hell go with it*. I am in a different space right now anyway.

He walks over to me and gives me a hug- I can't lie a lot of feelings I had for this man came rushing back. From all the laughs we had to how good he smelled. I remembered the first time we meet. Hell I remember the look he had on his face when I asked him to help me take a bath. Some feelings you can bury deep inside but when they finally get set free they are impossible to control... MERCY!!

We exchanged the normal small talk of, *how you been and what's going on?* He did shock me when he hit me with the, *he broke up with his girlfriend!*

I gave him the Scooby Doo, *Ruh-Roh?*!! A part of me was jumping for joy, but I would never let him know.

He was now looking at me in a very strange way. I felt like he wanted to tell me something but didn't know how. So, he comes out of nowhere and tells me that he has feelings for me.

It's been a month and now you realize that you have feelings for me? Now I am thinking what am I to do with this information? I honestly don't have an answer for him. I guess we are back to that 90 seconds of silence from before.

As much as I Love this man, I can't be the rebound chick. If he wants me he has to catch me.

I walk over to his bike gave him a long embrace. I look him in his eyes and kiss him -a soft, long, passionate kiss.

It was my version of the forehead kiss. It was a kiss that had meaning behind it.

Marcus was speechless. I liked him that way. I walked back to my bike and put on my helmet, my gloves, and started my bike. Before I took off I gave him the universal head nod. Then I did what any real biker would do. I looked both ways and took off.

In my mind I wasn't telling him no, but I wasn't jumping in his arms either. This past year and a half with this bike has taught me a lot. I lost myself in the bike world only to find myself again. I really just wanted to enjoy the ride. I don't care about patches, clubs, parties, or who's property of whom!!! Being with Marcus will not change that. So I am off to do just that and will always continue to… ENJOY THE RIDE!!!

Just as I take that breath of the view and the wind's in my helmet, I look into my mirror…whom do I see!?!